Dad Gummit & Ma Foot

by Karen Waggoner

illustrated by Anita Riggio

Orchard Books   New York

To Alan, Shemariah, and Eben, with love.
—K.W.

For old friends, dear friends, Mary Cay and Mary Grace,
with love and thanks to Alice Carlson Axelson.
—A. R.

Text copyright © 1990 by Karen Waggoner
Illustrations copyright © 1990 by Anita Riggio

ORCHARD BOOKS
A division of Franklin Watts, Inc.
387 Park Avenue South
New York, NY 10016

Manufactured in the United States of America
Printed by General Offset Company, Inc.
Bound by Horowitz/Rae
Book design by Jean Krulis

10 9 8 7 6 5 4 3 2 1

The text of this book is set in 15 pt. Janson
The illustrations are watercolors

Library of Congress Cataloging-in-Publication Data.
Waggoner, Karen. Dad Gummit and Ma Foot / by Karen Waggoner : illustrated by Anita Riggio. p. cm. Summary: After fifty years of estrangement following a quarrel, two sweethearts finally get together again with the help of a cow and blackberry patch.
ISBN 0-531-05891-3.—ISBN 0-531-08491-4 (lib. bdg.) [1. Quarreling—Fiction.] I. Riggio, Anita, ill. II. Title. PZ7.W12413Dad 1990
[E]—dc20 89-70983 CIP AC

Long ago, in the days when folks still lived on the lonesome side of the mountain, a young man and a young woman fell in love. They had eyes only for each other, and their sweet whispered words were heard by no one else.

Soon, everyone knew, Thomas and Clara would be married.
And what a handsome couple they made—she with her pearly pink

skin and raven hair, he with his deep brown eyes and wavy black beard.

But one day Thomas and Clara returned home from a church picnic with fiery eyes and fuming words.

"That fickle scamp of a boy!"
Clara wept to her mother.

"That snippy twit of a girl!"
Thomas complained to his father.

"Marriage?" cried Clara.
"Marriage, ma foot!"

"Dad gummit!" Thomas told his friends.
"There'll be no wedding!"

And no one knew why.
Thomas and Clara vowed never to see each other again.

Years went by. Others married, gave birth, moved away, or died. But Thomas and Clara were left alone, living their separate lives under their separate roofs, and getting more cantankerous with each passing year.

When Thomas went to town on Tuesdays and Clara on Saturdays, the townspeople saw two crotchety characters who seldom had a kind word for anyone, and *never* about each other. If Pearl Tate at Tate's Hardware remarked, "Must get kind of lonesome up on that mountain," Clara would grumble, "Lonesome for that fickle scamp of a boy? Lonesome, ma foot!"

If Hiram Peck at the feed store finished his commentary on the weather and said, "Clara was in the other day," Thomas would snort, "Suits me fine never to lay eyes on that snippy twit of a girl again, dad gummit!"

Before long nobody called Thomas and Clara anything but Dad Gummit and Ma Foot.

Dad Gummit told himself he was content with his cow, Claretta, who provided the sweet creamy milk he poured over his cornbread every night.

Ma Foot believed she was satisfied with the company of her orange cat, Tom, and with the sweetest patch of blackberries on the lonesome side of the mountain. Every evening she baked blackberry buckle.

When the mouth-watering scent of baking buckle floated on the evening breeze over to Dad Gummit's place, he slammed his windows shut. "Smells worse than boiled-to-death cabbage!" he muttered. But as he stared at his cornbread, he thought, "Sure would be nice to have something different to sop up Claretta's good milk. Dad gummit! That snippy twit of a girl probably doesn't appreciate her own buckle."

When the clear ring of Claretta's bell drifted on the morning breeze through Ma Foot's window, she covered her ears. "Sweet milk, ma foot! Likely it's sour," she told her cat, Tom. But to herself she said, "If it was anyone else's cow, I'd borrow a cup of something nice and creamy to pour over my buckle. 'Tis pure foolishness to waste good milk on that fickle scamp of a boy!"

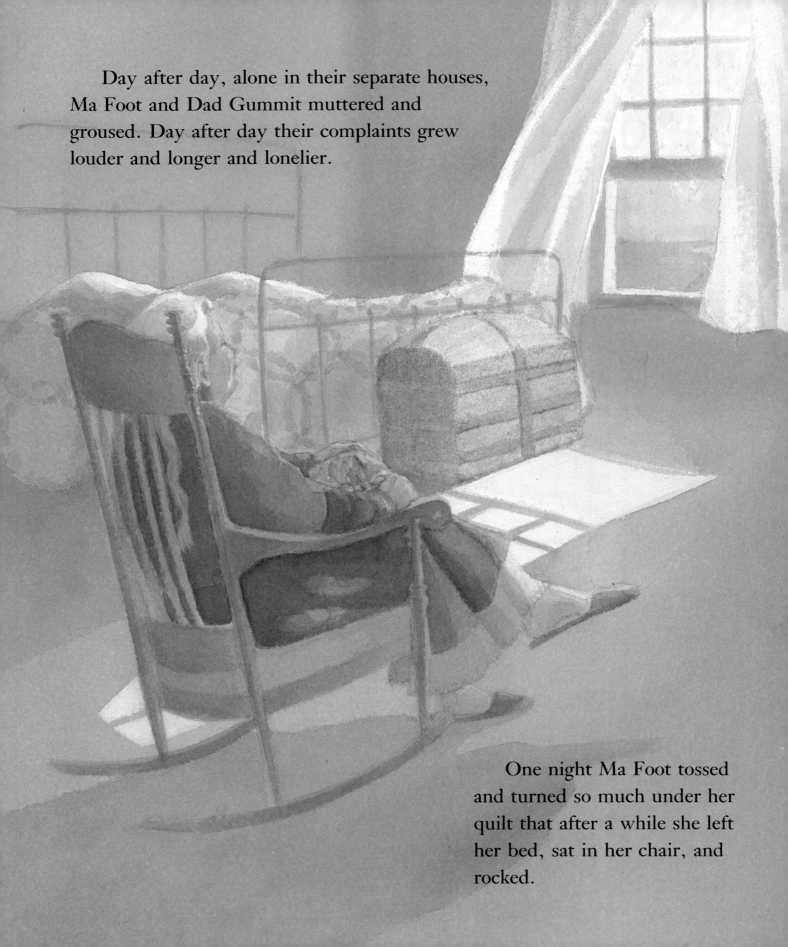

Day after day, alone in their separate houses, Ma Foot and Dad Gummit muttered and groused. Day after day their complaints grew louder and longer and lonelier.

One night Ma Foot tossed and turned so much under her quilt that after a while she left her bed, sat in her chair, and rocked.

That same night Dad Gummit couldn't sleep either,
so he went to the barn for a long talk with Claretta.

The next morning Ma Foot woke up an hour before the time she usually heard the clang of Claretta's bell. She took her blackberry pail and crept through her berry patch, through the wet grass of Claretta's pasture, and into the barn.

"Moo?" said Claretta, who always woke slowly.

"Moo yourself," said Ma Foot, and she milked Claretta dry.

Meanwhile, Dad Gummit rose at his usual milking hour. He took Claretta's pail and crept around the barn, through Claretta's pasture, to the thickest part of the blackberry patch, where he picked the bushes clean.

Dad Gummit was still chuckling when he returned to milk Claretta. As he entered the barn, he tripped over his milking stool, which was not hanging in its usual place on the wall.

"Dad gummit! Now what fool left this here for me to stumble over?" he muttered as he sat down beside his cow. When Claretta gave no milk, he asked, "Not feeling up to snuff, eh girl?" and scratched her ears.

Ma Foot was feeling mighty pleased with herself when she went to her blackberry patch that morning. But her mouth dropped open when she found all her berries gone. "Feathered friends, ma foot!" she said scowling at the treetops and blaming the birds. "And where'd this ugly thing blow in from?" she grouched as she grabbed a faded red handkerchief that had caught on a bush.

At day's end, Ma Foot had sweet creamy milk but no buckle to pour it over. She tried it on leftover cornbread. But it just wasn't tasty.

That same evening Dad Gummit sat down to fresh blackberry buckle, but he had to eat it dry. "Chews like sawdust," he said to himself. "Maybe I forgot the recipe."

Dad Gummit worried about Claretta's milk and rubbed the shin that had collided with that oddly out-of-place milking stool.

Ma Foot fretted about her blackberries and stared hard at the red handkerchief, which she had washed and hung with her herbs to dry.

Suddenly, they both knew what had happened.

Ma Foot hurried to a round-top chest at the end of her bed. Buried beneath some linens she'd embroidered with Thomas's initials fifty years earlier was a small silver picture frame. Inside were the same deep brown eyes and wavy black beard she remembered from fifty years before. "That fickle scamp of a boy!" she cried. "I should have returned this a long time ago!"

At the same time, Dad Gummit was pawing furiously through his wardrobe until he found the suit he'd bought a half century ago for a wedding that never took place. From an inside pocket he removed a picture in a round silver frame. He took one look and snorted, "Same raven hair and pearly pink skin. Same snippy twit of a girl she always was!" Why he'd kept her picture so long he couldn't imagine.

Ma Foot stomped through her berry patch, getting madder and madder at the scamp who'd picked them clean. Dad Gummit stormed across Claretta's meadow, furious at the twit who bothered his cow.

In the near dark they almost collided.
He was startled and cried out, "Dad gummit!"
"Ma foot!" she sputtered in surprise.

They stared at each other as strangers. There, facing Dad Gummit, was a plumpish old woman with wrinkly skin and silver gray hair. There, facing Ma Foot, was a wiry old man with crinkly eyes and a bushy white beard.

Dad Gummit felt the silver frame in his pocket. "Clara, you've changed," he said.

"So have you, Thomas," said Ma Foot, clutching her silver frame to her breast. "I'd invite you over, but I'm out of berries."

"And I'd invite you over, but my cow's sick," said Dad Gummit.
"Oh, no she's not," said Ma Foot.
"Don't I know it!" said Dad Gummit.
"Who was that girl I saw you kissing?" asked Ma Foot.
"*I* wasn't kissing anyone. *She* was kissing *me*. Would have told you that fifty years ago at the church picnic, but you wouldn't listen."

They stood silently as the moon
rose above the trees.

"We were young and foolish,"
Ma Foot said finally.
"Yup," said Dad Gummit.
"Now we're old and foolish."

Ma Foot smiled. "No need to stay that way, Thomas."

Dad Gummit wiped his hand on his pants and held it out. "No need at all, Clara, no need at all."